Hippo and Rabbit in

THREE SHORT TALES

Jeff Mack

Cartwheel
·B·O·O·K·S·®

SCHOLASTIC INC.

New York   Toronto   London   Auckland
Sydney   Mexico City   New Delhi   Hong Kong

—Table of— CONTENTS

Hey Kellie, can you look at this?
—J. M.

All rights reserved. Published by Scholastic Inc.
SCHOLASTIC, CARTWHEEL BOOKS, and associated logos
are trademarks and/or registered trademarks of Scholastic Inc.
Lexile is a registered trademark of MetaMetrics, Inc.

Hand-lettering & design by Angela Navarra
Text hand-lettering by Jeff Mack

Library of Congress Cataloging-in-Publication Data

Mack, Jeff.
Hippo & Rabbit in three short tales / by Jeff Mack.
p. cm. -- (Scholastic reader. Level 1)
Summary: Friends Hippo and Rabbit spend the day together having
breakfast, playing on the swings, and waiting for a thunderstorm to end.
ISBN 978-0-545-27445-6 (pbk.)
[1. Friendship--Fiction. 2. Hippopotamus--Fiction. 3.
Rabbits--Fiction.] I. Title. II. Title: Hippo and Rabbit in three short tales. III. Series.

PZ7.M18973Hi 2011
[E]--dc22

2010013567

ISBN 978-0-545-27445-6

10 9 8 7 6 5 4 3 2 1   11 12 13 14/0

Printed in the U.S.A. 40
First printing, January 2011

4

6

SWING

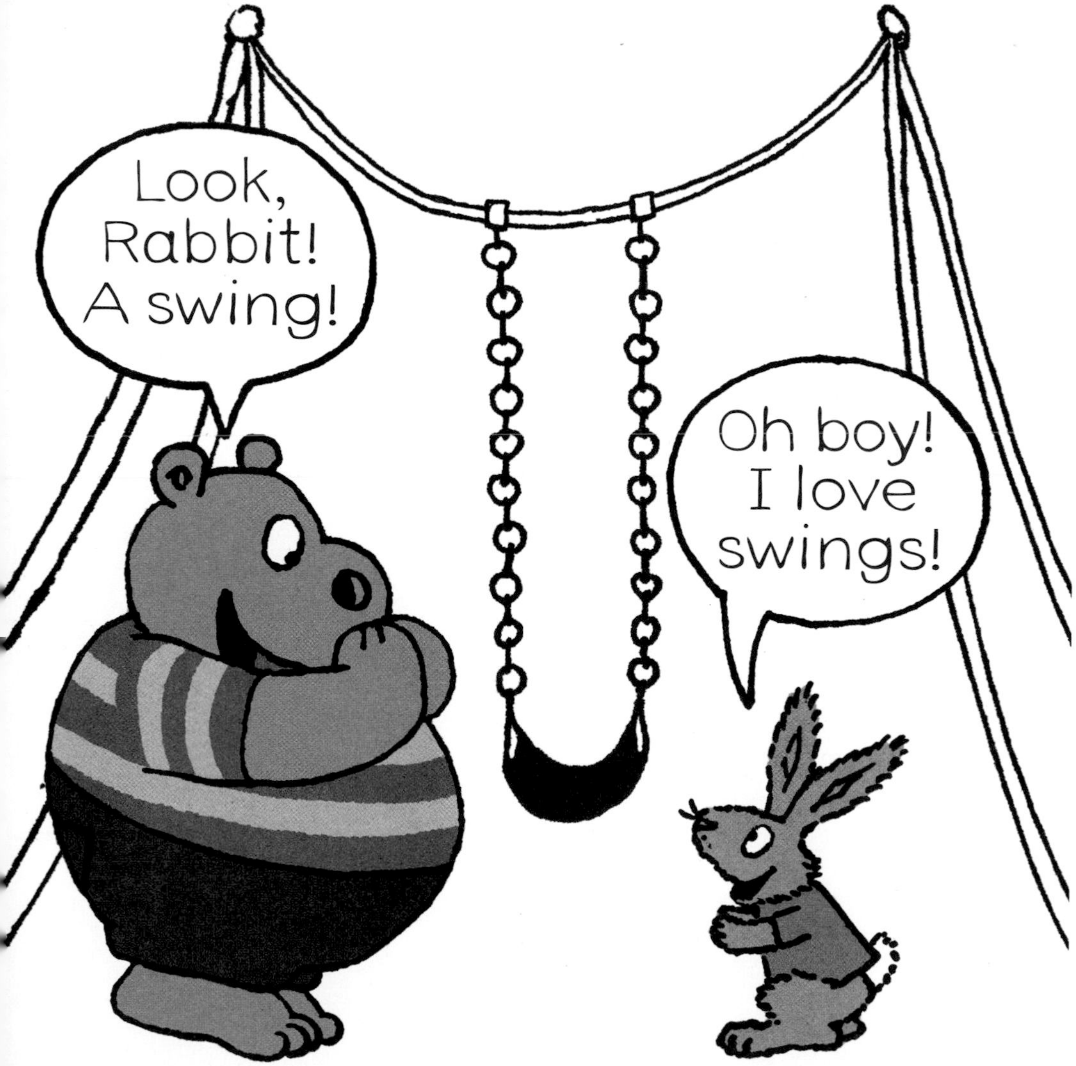

19

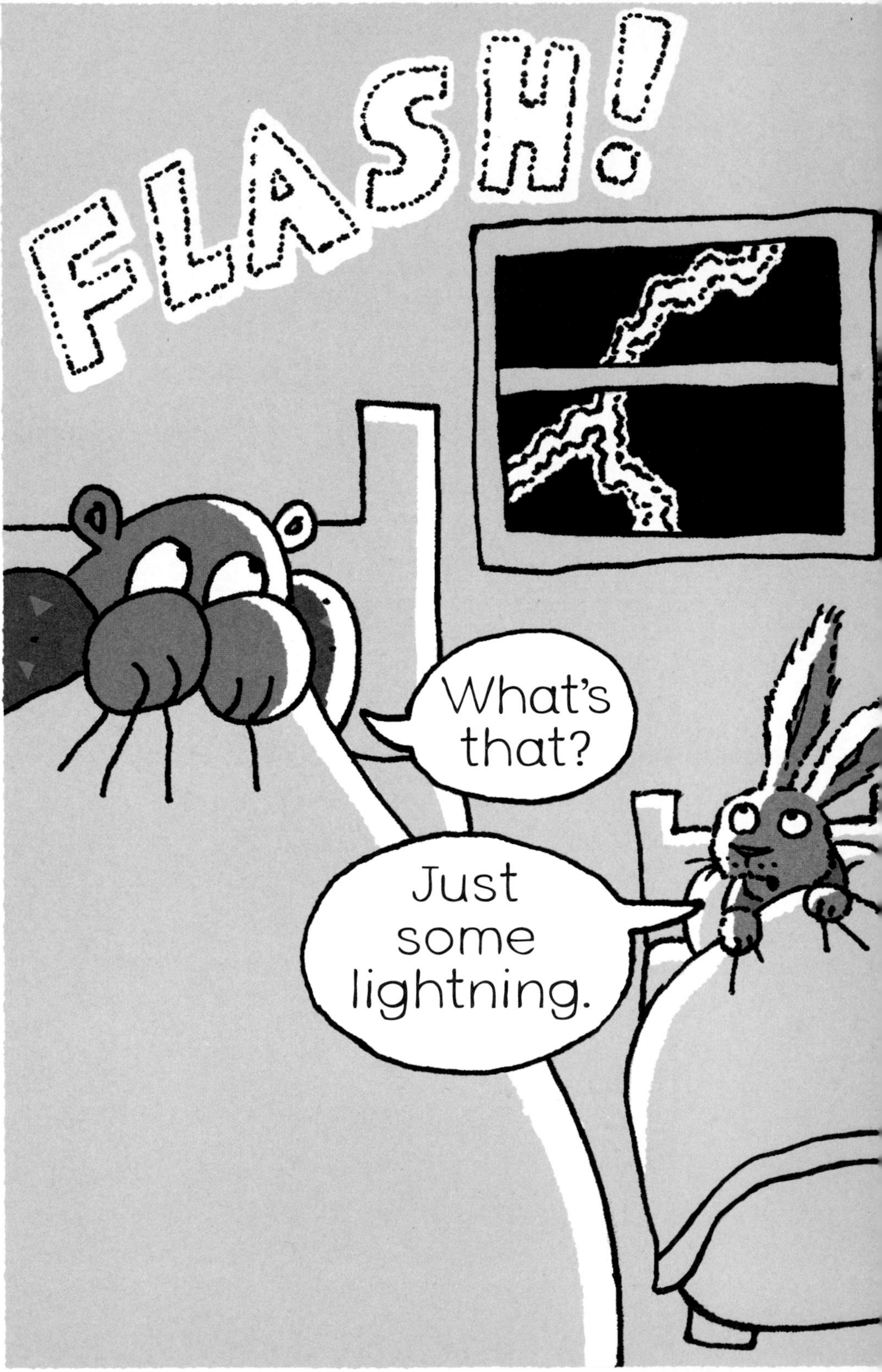
FLASH!
What's that?
Just some lightning.

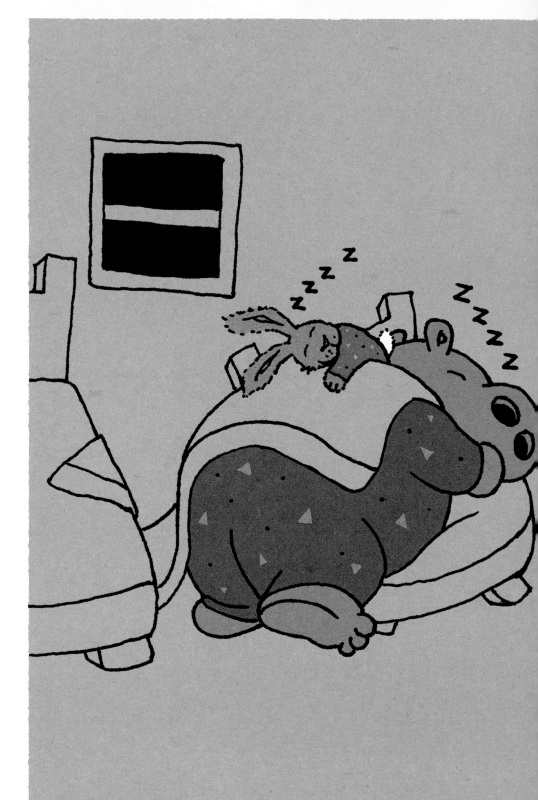